# The Great Book of Fantastic Creatures

by Giuseppe D'Anna

Illustrated by Anna Láng

STERLING CHILDREN'S BOOKS

New York

# Contents

# Introduction

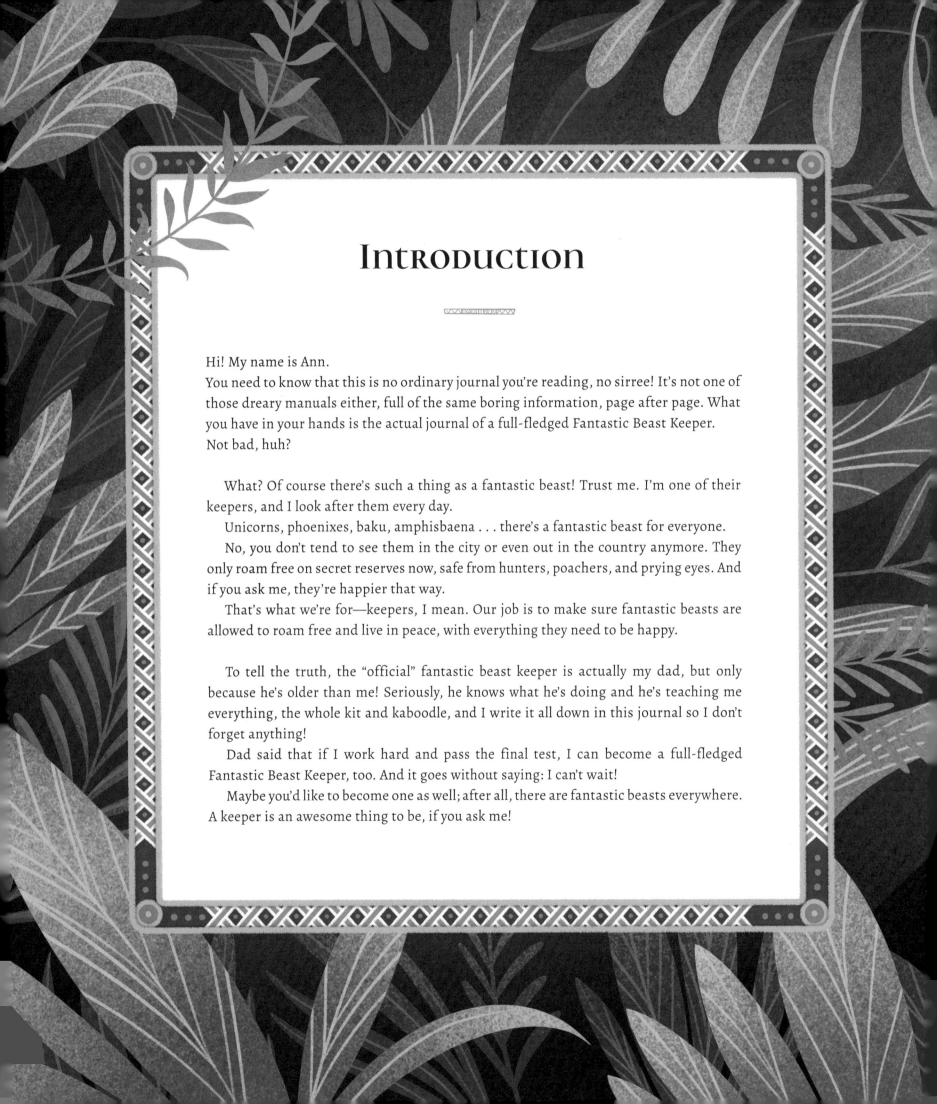

Hi! My name is Ann.

You need to know that this is no ordinary journal you're reading, no sirree! It's not one of those dreary manuals either, full of the same boring information, page after page. What you have in your hands is the actual journal of a full-fledged Fantastic Beast Keeper. Not bad, huh?

What? Of course there's such a thing as a fantastic beast! Trust me. I'm one of their keepers, and I look after them every day.

Unicorns, phoenixes, baku, amphisbaena . . . there's a fantastic beast for everyone.

No, you don't tend to see them in the city or even out in the country anymore. They only roam free on secret reserves now, safe from hunters, poachers, and prying eyes. And if you ask me, they're happier that way.

That's what we're for—keepers, I mean. Our job is to make sure fantastic beasts are allowed to roam free and live in peace, with everything they need to be happy.

To tell the truth, the "official" fantastic beast keeper is actually my dad, but only because he's older than me! Seriously, he knows what he's doing and he's teaching me everything, the whole kit and kaboodle, and I write it all down in this journal so I don't forget anything!

Dad said that if I work hard and pass the final test, I can become a full-fledged Fantastic Beast Keeper, too. And it goes without saying: I can't wait!

Maybe you'd like to become one as well; after all, there are fantastic beasts everywhere. A keeper is an awesome thing to be, if you ask me!

# Fantastic Beasts
## FOR Trainee Keepers

Cool! If you've turned the page, it means you want to become a Fantastic Beast Keeper, too. So, let's see. You could start by learning from my dad, just like me.

Lesson number one: there are lots of different beasts, and you won't find many cuddly, friendly ones. In fact, they're anything but . . .

Don't worry, though. In this first part of my journal, I've only included fantastic beasts for Trainee Keepers—the tamer ones that are easier to approach. So no sharp fangs, poisonous quills, or tongues of fire.

That doesn't mean they won't get angry with you if you're not careful! All beasts, just like ordinary animals, can be dangerous in their own way.

So, keep your eyes open and trust your instincts, okay?

# Unicorn
## Classification: Equine

No doubt you've already heard of this one. It's called *unicorn* in English, but other countries have different names for it, like licorne in France and liocorno in Italy.

No matter what you call it, don't expect it to reply to you or come anywhere near you. Unicorns are very timid creatures and easily scared. They only let young girls near them, or children who smile at them and are kind (which I'm very good at, speaking modestly!).

Oh, and don't forget that it will never, ever let you on its back. That's why you'll never read a story with a courageous knight or a dashing prince riding a unicorn!

It's easy to tell unicorns apart from an ordinary horse: just look at their forehead. If there's a large horn projecting out of the middle of it, then you're looking at a unicorn! The horn is also the reason unicorns flee from humans. You've no idea how many wizards would like to put these horns into their magic potions.

The spiraling horn resembles a corkscrew (only much bigger)!

The coat is so white it shines in the dark.

Unicorns might look like horses, but if you take a closer look, the beard and hooves are the same as a goat's!

## Favorite Pastimes:

Roaming around the forest looking for obstacles to jump. Unicorns are very good at this but have to be careful not to get their horn tangled up in the branches!

## How to Attract a Unicorn:

Unicorns love music but only if it's not too loud, so no loudspeakers or microphones. The best thing would be to play a flute or guitar. If you don't play a musical instrument yet, you can always try whistling a tune!

## How to Make Friends with a Unicorn:

• Offer it some sugar cubes (they love them, just like horses!). But not too many, though—it might make the unicorn sick . . . or ruin its teeth!

• The mane needs to be brushed very gently and, if you can, try to braid it, too. Unicorns like to look tidy.

• Never climb on its back, not even as a joke (would you like someone to climb up on your shoulders?!).

There's also a very rare species of winged unicorn, called an alicorn. Its magnificent wings are layered with feathers, like those of a swan.

# Baku

CLASSIFICATION: NOCTURNAL HYBRID

If you have frequent nightmares or often feel a little unlucky, the baku could be your ideal fantastic beast.

This giant tapir-like animal with the body of a bear and paws of a tiger feeds on bad dreams, bad luck, and evil spirits. It sucks them up into its tiny trunk and swallows them down like candies, leaving you to go peacefully back to sleep or to whatever you were doing, with nothing more to fear. Problem solved (or almost!).

When you wake up after a nightmare, scared, and you think there's someone in your bedroom, don't worry: it's probably just a baku having a snack. Shout "thank you" at the top of your lungs, and the next night you'll be assured much sweeter dreams!

With padded paws, the baku is soft-footed and very silent (so as not to wake sleeping children!).

The nightmare-sucking trunk looks just like the short one tapirs have.

A baku often has a sleepy look on its face; you would think it spends the whole day napping!

## Favorite Pastimes:

Hiding under children's beds or in their closets to protect them from bad dreams (and have a tasty feast!).

## How to Attract a Baku:

- Offer it a soft pillow to lie down on. Being on its feet all night can be pretty exhausting.

- Scratch the base of its trunk, right between the eyes. It's the only part it can't reach by itself.

- If you come across a baku fast asleep in a bush during the day, don't wake it up!

It is said that a famous samurai called Toyotomi Hideyoshi used to sleep with a picture of a baku under his pillow, to ward off nightmares.

# Carbuncle

CLASSIFICATION: NOCTURNAL RODENT

*Glowing* is probably the best word to describe this fantastic rodent, as the gemstone set in its forehead glows like a flame in the dark. And that's not all! An equally bright, bluish light shines out from under its shell (maybe it has other precious stones tucked away under there, but no one has ever found them!).

Luckily, a carbuncle's shell can also close into a ball, making it look like a stone on the ground that gem hunters won't notice and will walk on past (leaving the carbuncle's treasure alone!).

You won't be surprised to learn that carbuncles are said to like hiding treasure. They must be pretty good at it, too. After all, no one has ever managed to find any gems near a carbuncle's den. Oh, how do you recognize a carbuncle's den? Easy. It's the only one that shines in the dark!

Carbuncles have a long tail and when they're pretending to be a stone, the tail sometimes gives them away. There's always a little bit that sticks out!

The gemstone on a carbuncle's forehead can tell you a lot about it. The more it shines, the happier it is.

Even its tiny talons, which it keeps nice and sharp for digging, are shiny.

## Favorite Pastimes:

Digging holes furtively in the forest.
Who knows if they're digging to find treasure
. . . or to hide it?!

## How to Attract a Carbuncle:

One very apt word to describe a carbuncle is vain.
Dad says you can use a mirror as bait: the carbuncle
will jump out from wherever it's hiding to come and
admire its reflection.

When a carbuncle feels in danger and its shell is not enough protection, it has a secret weapon: the light from the gemstone on its forehead shines so bright it can blind anyone coming near it, giving it time to scurry away to safety.

## How to Make Friends with a Carbuncle:

• Offer to polish its stone with a soft cloth (remember to be gentle—you don't want to scratch it!).

• Leave something as sparkly as it near its den. This can be a stone, a piece of glass, anything. As long as it's shiny! I often use marbles.

• Don't knock on its shell while it's closed up in a ball. It's probably tired or scared and doesn't want to be disturbed.

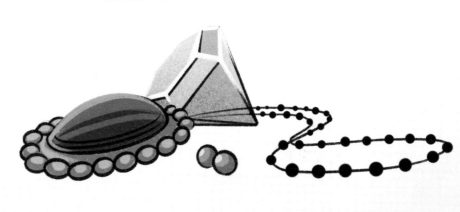

# Alicanto
## Classification: Metal Eater Bird

An alicanto is a bird, but it can't fly. I know that's not great for a bird, but ostriches have the same problem. Essentially, its wings are be big enough, but alicantos are very partial to eating gold, silver, and other precious metals, and with all that parked in their stomachs, it's no wonder they're too heavy to get off the ground!

An alicanto's feathers glimmer with gold or silver hues depending on what metal it has eaten.

If you'd like to see one, you'll have to join the long line of miners and treasure hunters constantly on this extraordinary creature's trail, convinced of the rich new deposits they'll uncover when they finally catch a carbuncle! Think carefully, though, before you spend any time tracking it: if an alicanto realizes it's being followed, it'll lead you straight into a dead end. Or worse still, get you stuck in a rock crevice!

An alicanto might not be able to fly, but it can run like the wind on its long, powerful legs!

Watch out for the alicanto's beak! To eat metal without injuring itself, the beak has to be equally tough.

# Hippalectryon
## Classification: Equine

If you take the front of a horse and the hindquarters of a rooster (wings included!), what you end up with is a hippalectryon.

It may strike great fear in those encountering it, but, unlike unicorns, hippalectryons will allow themselves to be ridden on one condition: if the aspiring rider is considered worthy.

The hippalectryon's call is said to drive evil away, like the call of an ordinary rooster drives away the night to make room for the day.

There are very few myths about this funny-looking steed (that's probably why you've never heard of it), but it appears as a decoration on some ancient vases and plates (no, not the ones in your grandmother's china cabinet—much older than that!).

In ancient times, they were painted on the sails of warships to keep sailors safe and to defeat their enemies.

The hippalectryon's magnificent tail serves as a powerful rudder, enabling it to steer right or left with a lightning flap!

Watch out for the hind legs: the hippalectryon kicks like a horse, and its talons are as sharp as a rooster's!

# Thunderbird
## Classification: Nocturnal Flying Animal

Would you believe it if I told you that horrible scary
thunderstorms are caused by a giant bird of prey?
Well, you should, because it's true.

Thunderbirds flap their enormous wings, heaping all the
clouds in the sky on top of each other into a massive cumulus
that gets darker and darker. Even the menacing rumble you
hear during a thunderstorm is caused by their wings endlessly
beating!

What else? Ah yes, flashes of lightning are luminous serpents
falling from its mouth mid-flight (how they get them nobody
knows!).

Come to think of it, I'm not sure you'll be any less frightened
now, knowing there's an enormous bird hiding up there.

Open your arms wide and stretch out
your fingers . . . there, that's how long a
thunderbird's feather is!

24

A thunderbird's curved horns are perfect for diving headfirst into clouds that are ready to pop with rain!

Not only do thunderbirds have razor-sharp claws and beaks, but they also have dangerously pointed teeth.

## Favorite Pastimes:

Causing storms for the sake of it—especially on the weekend, when people are ready to go to the beach or on a picnic!

## How to Attract a Thunderbird:

Dad says that big birds need big nests! Find some long branches or very broad leaves and lay them out in plain sight when the sky clouds over. Rest assured a thunderbird will swoop past to thank you and snatch up the very welcome gifts!

## How to Make Friends with a Thunderbird:

• All birds like to crack nuts with their beaks, but you need to find a particular kind of nut for such a large bird. Say, a coconut?

• Give him a soft, cozy scarf—it's always so cold in the middle of a storm!

• Never open an umbrella near a thunderbird! It would be like saying you don't like his storms . . . an unforgivable insult.

Many people have reported seeing a thunderbird, but no one has ever been able to prove it or, better yet, catch one. Apparently, thunderbirds are not good at staying hidden but, when they're spotted, they can zip away . . . in a flash!

# Fantastic Beasts
## FOR EXPERT KEEPERS

Hello there!

Have you read all the way through the first part of my journal already? Really? You didn't skip a few pages along the way?

I'm only asking because, before you read on, it's imperative that you are now a proper Trainee Keeper able to root out an alicanto or catch a baku in the blink of an eye.

Does that sound like you?

Great! You're ready to move on to the second part of my journal now.

It's time to talk about fantastic beasts for Expert Keepers.

Yes, that means the really dangerous ones. And by "dangerous," I mean creatures that sting, bite, crush, or poison anyone they don't like! (Sometimes it doesn't take much, but you'll find that out later.)

In any case, no need to be afraid. Part of becoming an Expert Keeper also means learning how not to become a chimera's next meal!

# Phoenix
## Classification: Ancient Flying Animal

The phoenix is one of the most striking fantastic beasts you could ever meet. But beware: they're also one of the most dangerous.

Indeed, there's more to fear than just its beak or its golden talons. At any time, even while you're stroking it, it could ignite and leave you in a ring of towering, golden flames of a kind you've never seen before!

Some people say you can ride a flying phoenix if you hold on tight to the two long feathers at the back of its head. I wouldn't risk it, though.

A phoenix's vision is almost as sharp as its talons.

Watch out for the phoenix's talons: they shine like gemstones but are as sharp as knives!

But don't worry: this ancient creature always rises from its ashes, reborn, stronger and more beautiful than ever. That's why it doesn't think twice about self-combusting when it feels threatened, angry, or annoyed (or even just bored). Watching a phoenix go up in flames is a little like watching a fireworks display in the starry sky: awesome!

## Favorite Pastimes:

Flying to the highest peaks, then soaring and taking in everything around them, thanks to their perfect vision. That's why phoenixes know everything about everything (remember that!).

## How to Approach a Phoenix:

These amazing creatures can live for hundreds of years, so don't be surprised if you meet one and it seems a tad old-fashioned. A bow and a polite gesture are the best ways to win it over. Always greet it with a "good morning" and never raise your voice in its presence.

## How not to Make a Phoenix Angry:

• Phoenixes like herbs (thyme and lavender, for example). Try to find some for its nest.

• If a phoenix approaches you, stick out your arm for it to perch on and have a rest (watch out, it's heavy!).

• No, you can't use a phoenix's flames to cook marshmallows or make popcorn (unless you're very good at dodging sharp pecks)!

When a phoenix decides to regenerate, it normally does so from the comfort of its nest, a special one woven out of branches and herbs into a sort of egg. That's when it goes up in flames, like a bonfire (which, for a phoenix, feels like a cold shower in summer).

# Cerberus
## Classification: Watchdog

If you're not fond of dogs, then you might have a few issues with this beast, given that a cerberus is like three mastiffs in one! No, really, that wasn't a joke: a cerberus has one tail, four legs, and three heads—each more ferocious than the next.

Clearly, a cerberus would make the perfect guard dog. Three heads means three pairs of eyes peering in every direction, three pairs of ears to hear every noise, and three noses all aquiver, smelling everything in the air!

Unfortunately, the cerberus isn't quite as talented when it comes to retrieving sticks that I throw, as the three heads can't agree which one of them should bring the stick back . . .

The drool of a cerberus isn't poisonous and doesn't sting, but it is very, very sticky! Yuck!

The cerberus has a coat as black as night, perfect for hiding in the shadows.

There's no denying how frightening a cerberus's teeth are, but the toenails are nothing to sniff at, either!

## Favorite Pastimes

Picking a spot to watch over (a corridor or an entrance to a cave is ideal) and not letting anyone past until . . . well, until it says so!

## How to Approach a Cerberus:

The weak spot of a cerberus is its stomach (with three mouths, that's three ways in!). It never refuses food, and you'll find it a lot meeker after gulping down a tasty leg of lamb or a string of sausages.

## How not to Make a Cerberus Angry:

• It has one ear that it likes to receive the occasional tickle behind, but the problem is working out which ear it is, given that there are six . . .

• Before you approach it, make sure you're not too sweaty or wearing too much perfume (all three of its noses hate strong smells!).

• Dad always says, "Let sleeping dogs lie." I like to add, "Especially if they have three heads and a nasty disposition."

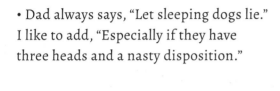

The bark of a cerberus is so deep and booming it sends everyone running (trust me, it's worse than a crash of thunder!).

# Hydra

## Classification: Poisonous Reptile

Be warned: this fantastic beast is not one of the nicest.

In addition to resembling a giant serpent with legs, it can poison you with its bite, its breath, and even with the tracks it leaves on the ground (that's right, careful where you put your feet)!

As if that weren't bad enough, it has nine heads, all equally poisonous and each one ready to bite you if you get too close.

When a legendary hero of the past called Hercules came up against one of these creatures, he decided that the best course of action was to "cut himself some slack"—which he did, literally, severing all nine heads at once! In so doing, he discovered that the hydra is able to regenerate its severed heads, just like a lizard regrows its tail (although lizards don't try to eat you afterward)!

Oh, I almost forgot: don't let it wrap its tail around you! It might crush you!

Hydras have vertical pupils, which means they can see much better at night (so I recommend you approach it during the day!).

Hydras can pick up scents with their tongues, just like snakes. If it moves too quickly, it means it can smell something (and that something could be you!).

There's no point trying to threaten a hydra or give it orders; it won't hear anything you say, although it can pick up vibrations in the ground (so forget sneaking up behind one: it'll hear you coming!).

## Favorite Pastimes:

Hiding at the bottom of lakes, staying cool until
the next hero to fight comes along.

## How to Approach a Hydra:

To hold off a hydra, run circles around it as fast as
you can, first in one direction and then in the other!
If you can confuse its many heads, they'll end up in
a tangle. I've done it many times!

## How not to Make a Hydra Angry:

• No sudden gestures! Hydras see everything that moves, and they don't like it when anything moves too fast.

• If I were you, I wouldn't go near a hydra with a crocodile skin bag or in snakeskin boots (they might have been cousins!).

• Be careful where you put your feet. Trampling a hydra's tail is an excellent way to infuriate all of its heads at the same time!

If you ever see a hydra sitting quietly, and not moving . . . well, let me tell you, it's probably not a hydra! Or not a whole one, anyway. It's almost certainly only the skin the hydra left behind after molting. Yes, hydras cast off their skin as they grow, the same way you change your clothes, only hydras don't pay any attention to where they leave them—yuck!

# Kitsune
## Classification: Ancient Canine

Many people like to say they're as "wily as a fox," but Dad always tells me it would be far better to be as "wily as a kitsune"!

It's this very wiliness that makes the kitsune such a dangerous fantastic beast.

No, it's not really evil. It's just a naughty prankster and incredibly cantankerous. Oh, and sneakily good at deception. Better not make it angry!

At first sight, you might think the kitsune looks just like an ordinary fox, but if you look again, you'll see it has one too many of something and that would be . . . tails! The older a kitsune, the more tails it has—up to nine in some cases.

What's more, a kitsune with nine tails is scarily powerful. When it rubs all of them together, leaping flames and fires can ensue (so once again, best not anger it; you've been warned!).

On gaining its ninth tail, the kitsune's skin turns white or gold.

A kitsune's ears are always pricked, and it has razor-sharp hearing!

The kitsune has such a penetrating gaze that some people say it can see what's happening in other places (even in other times!).

## Favorite Pastimes:

Making fun of humans and any other creatures it encounters in the woods. It might send you the wrong way or even lay a fake trail to throw you off track. It thinks it's very funny!

## How to Approach a Kitsune:

Kitsunes are highly intelligent creatures and adore the challenge that a bit of trickery presents. If you don't want to get caught up in one of their ruses, keep them busy by asking them to solve an unsolvable riddle. Or maybe ask them what a raven and a writing desk have in common . . .

## How not to Make a Kitsune Angry:

• If you don't know how old the kitsune is, whatever you do, don't treat it like a young pup. No "lil' mouse," "baby," or the like. It could be several hundred years old for all you know, and if it feels slighted, there'll be trouble!

• Don't let it see you irritated. If you fall for one of its ploys, try to laugh it off. Having a giggle about it is always going to be better than getting angry!

• Never play a trick on a kitsune! They can be very touchy and can get quite vindictive, which is why you should definitely try not to be.

Some nine-tailed kitsunes will try to pull an even funnier trick or deception (for them!) by shape-shifting into a young woman or an old man.
They can't get rid of their tails, however, so if you think you're looking at a kitsune-turned-human, check whether there's anything hairy popping out of its clothes!

# Griffin
## Classification: Flying Hybrid

The griffin is another hybrid creature, made up of two different animals (like the hippalectryon, remember?). It has the head, front feet, and wings of an eagle, and the hind legs and tail of a lion.

Do you know that means? That this fantastic beast is as smart as an eagle and as strong as a lion. It's agile up high in the sky and across the most rugged of terrains, easily navigating rocks and trees. That's why it's not a good idea to upset a griffin: you'd have nowhere to hide (not even under your bed!).

The good news is that griffins are not aggressive at all if they don't feel threatened. But don't think they're easy to mount; griffins are wild creatures that like to roam free (and it's only right they should be allowed to—a good keeper knows that!).

Some say griffins have a serpent for a tail, but that's not true! That would make it a chimera (more about that later)!

A griffin has two long and very beautiful feathered ears on its head.

# Ahuizotl

## Classification: Semiaquatic Hybrid

If you ever need a hand getting out of the water, don't ask
an ahuizotl! Despite having five hands (including one on
the end of its tail!), it would definitely use all of them to
drag you down to the bottom.

I don't think it does so to be mean. Maybe it just wants
to invite you home—which will always be a watery cavern at
the bottom of a river or lake—and forgets that not everyone
can hold their breath that long! So, be warned, you need to
be very careful when you bump into an ahuizotl, especially
if there's a lot of water around.

Wriggling out of its grip (or catching it, for that matter)
is an almost impossible task: it has the smooth, slippery
body of an eel, meaning it is a master at slithering away.

Never take your eyes off an ahuizotl's long
tail—the hand on the end is what it uses to
catch its prey.

# Peluda

## Classification: Poisonous Beast

The peluda is on the list of fantastic beasts I'd rather not meet. It's no laughing matter.

Don't be fooled by the thick, green fur—it might look like the soft fuzz of a cuddly toy, but it actually hides loads of deadly poisonous quills (never stroke a peluda, not even with a single finger!).

It has skin as hard as stone, tough enough to resist the attack of a hundred swords. There's just one vulnerable point, at the base of its tail, and this is what fantastic beast hunters all aim for! However, the peluda knows how to defend itself—it usually spits fire. But if it gets too hot, it likes to dive into the river and puff itself up into an enormous hairy balloon, causing the river to flood. Imagine that!

A peluda's much-feared poisonous quills can be as long as walking sticks.

The peluda gets its name from its shaggy coat. It's called the velue in French, and pelosa in Italian. Both names mean hairy one.

A peluda's stout, powerful feet are like those of a turtle.

# Chimera
## Classification: Poisonous Hybrid

You may have come across the word *chimera* in a book at some point, where it was used to describe an impossible dream. Do you know why? The chimera is such a strange creature that it almost seems impossible—although it's more like a nightmare than a dream. It has two grim heads: one a lion with razor-sharp fangs, and the other a goat, with two very sharp horns.

And then it has a poisonous snake for a tail!

Have I already told you that the lion's head breathes fire? Well, jot it down somewhere because it could take you by surprise and it always hits the target with its fiery breath. Oh, and you should also note that the breath of the goat's head could dry grass.

As I said, a real nightmare!

The chimera might have a goat's head, but the body is still that of a lion, so you won't get any goat's milk from it!

Like ordinary lions,
only male chimeras
have a mane.

# Amphisbaena
## Classification: Poisonous Reptile

Some amphisbaenas have small curved horns on both heads

Dad always says that "two heads are better than one," but I wouldn't say that for this creature. I don't know about you, but when I hear talk of poisonous snakes, I'm much happier when they only have one head.

Some keepers are convinced that only one of the amphisbaena's two heads are poisonous. That's not much help, though, as both heads are identical, making it difficult to work out which one is which. For safety's sake, I just try to make sure I don't get bitten by either head. I recommend you do the same!

Remember that this beast can dart as fast as lightning, left, right, forward, and back, and for the amphisbaena, it doesn't seem to matter which head goes first!

When one head sleeps, the other remains alert, scanning for enemies or undesirables. So don't think you can take it by surprise!

Unlike other serpents, the amphisbaena is a warm-blooded animal, so you might see it leap out at you in colder climes as well!

An amphisbaena's eyes glow like lanterns in the dark.

# THE KEEPER'S MINI GUIDE

Did you think you'd finished?

I'm afraid you're not quite done yet.

You might now know every fantastic beast there is (or the ones that my dad told me about!), but it doesn't mean you're a full-fledged keeper yet.

Do you know the five golden rules of a good keeper? Can you read the tracks of each of the beasts? Do you know which ones go wandering in the dead of night?

I've learned them all and you can, too, if you read this third (and final) part of my journal. After that, your apprenticeship will be complete!

# The Five Golden Rules

## of a Good Fantastic Beast Keeper

 ### 1  Fantastic beasts are not toys.

Even though you're their keeper and you treat them well, there's no saying they'll do everything you want. Just like other animals, fantastic beasts have their own mind, and they might not always feel like playing (so don't insist, okay?).

 ### 2  To Each their own food.

Why do fantastic beasts have to like the same food as you? Yes, it would certainly be easier, but it doesn't work like that (chips are not the right snack for a kitsune, trust me!).

Clearly, the opposite is true as well: a gold nugget would be a tasty treat for an alicanto, but it would cause you no end of problems, so don't eat the things you give the beasts. If you're not sure, always ask an adult before you offer food to an animal.

 ### 3  Never interrupt a beast while it's eating.

No one likes to be bothered while they're having dinner, whether they're a hydra, a carbuncle, or my uncle, who's great but to be avoided when he has his mouth full.

And never try to take food away from a beast, unless you want it to bite you instead!

 ### 4  Fantastic beasts need to be kept clean.

I know, I don't like picking up griffin poop, either! And I'll leave it to your imagination the fun and games trying to bathe a cerberus can be (note: I usually distract it with a couple of slices of ham). In any case, there's no excuse. If you want to be a keeper, you have to look after your beasts and keep them and their dens clean.

 ### 5  Always be on guard.

I know I've already said this, but I think it needs repeating. All beasts are dangerous in their own way, even the ones that seem harmless!

Take the unicorn, for instance. There's no denying it's as sweet as can be, but its hooves are rock hard. If a unicorn were to tread on your foot, say, you'd be left hopping on the other one for a good long time. It happened to me once.

So, keep your eyes open and reflexes at the ready!

# On the Fantastic Beast Trail:

## Can You Identify Their Tracks?

"Sometimes, the answer you're looking for is right under your nose."

Dad says this to me all the time, and when he's talking about tracks,
I have to admit he's right.
If you want to learn something about a creature, there's nothing more useful
than studying the tracks it leaves on the ground.
Do you think that sounds weird? Well, it's not!
You have no idea how many things (three for sure, all equally important) you can learn!

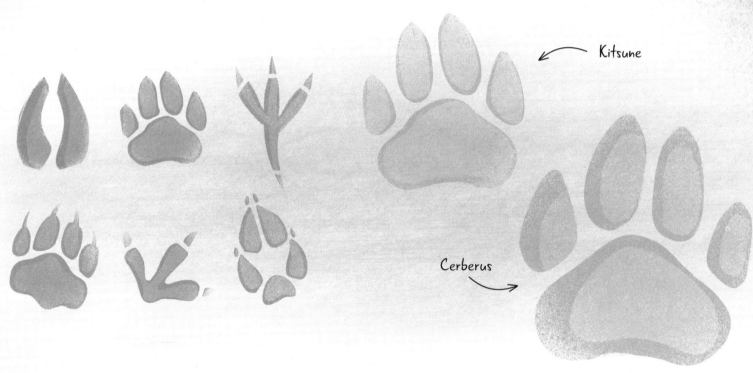

Kitsune

Cerberus

## One

For starters, you can see which creature the tracks belong to, because every fantastic beast has an unusual kind of foot and every foot leaves its own distinct footprint. So, before you do anything else, study the feet of each fantastic beast in detail. Afterward, you'll find it easy to recognize their tracks. Unicorns, for example, leave the same hoof prints as a horse, right? No! If you look back over my notes, you'll see that unicorn hooves resemble those of a goat, so their tracks will be like a goat's (only bigger!).

## Two

From the track left on the ground, you can tell how heavy the creature is (so how big it is!).
The deeper the track, the heavier the fantastic beast that left it.
The kitsune and cerberus, you might have noticed, have similar feet, yet the tracks of a cerberus are much, much deeper. The three heads tend to weigh it down a lot!

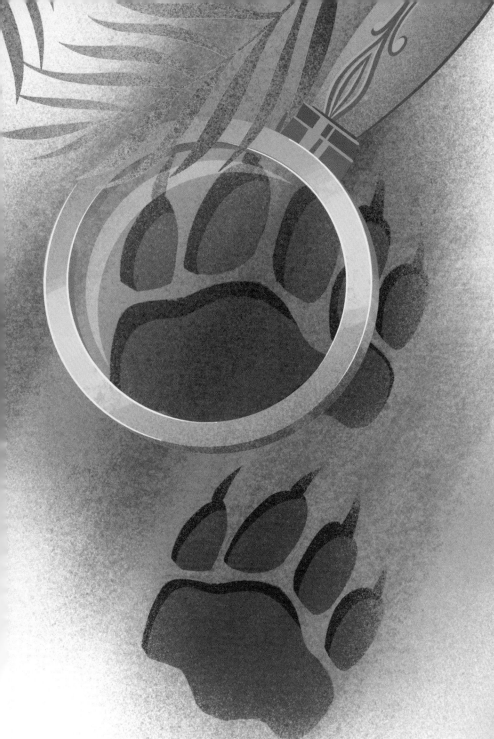

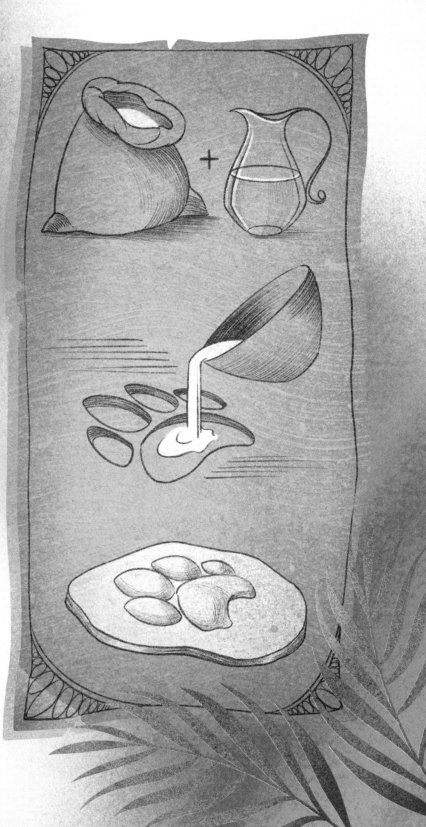

A little trick I found really useful at the beginning of my training was to take a cast of any footprints I came across. It means you'll always have it, to study and look at whenever you want!

How does it work? It's easy. Just get some chalk, mix it with water, pour it into the footprint, and wait for it to harden. Piece of cake!

## Three

Something else you could learn from an animal's tracks is whether it was running or just roaming around peacefully. If the tracks on the ground are clean and you can clearly make out the shape, then it was walking. If they're not very deep and are a little messed up, it was probably running as fast as it could. What was that? You'd rather not know why? I'm with you on that one!

# Who's Afraid of the Dark?

## Creatures you Might Meet at Night

Let's get one thing clear—never go walking around by yourself in the dark.
Not in a hidden reserve full of fantastic beasts.
I'm not kidding.
It could be extremely dangerous (when it's dark, I only ever go out with my dad).
In any case, it's always better to know which fantastic beasts might be awake and bursting
with energy in the dead of night.

Make no bones about it: when the moon is out and the sky is as black as ink, you could easily meet a **baku** out hunting for bad dreams. You know it's not dangerous, but if you bump into one, best not make any noise. When it's out hunting for the nightmares it feeds on, the baku always hangs out around other sleeping creatures—and they *would* be dangerous if you wake them!

The **cerberus** also prefers to go hunting at night. Its black coat makes a great camouflage (meaning it keeps it hidden), and being so dark, the cerberus looks like just another of the many shadows. So, if you see an odd-looking shadow, foaming like a mastiff (or like three mastiffs) in the middle of the night, watch out!

If you happen to glimpse something silver or gold glowing in the dark, there has to be an **alicanto** in the vicinity. Given all the treasure hunters constantly on its trail, it's not surprising that this fantastic bird prefers to move around at night. Maybe it hopes it won't be seen, although its glorious plumage makes that difficult!

Finally, there's the **amphisbaena**: not very pleasant to meet but, luckily, very easy to avoid.
If you've been paying attention, you'll remember that this twin-headed serpent has eyes that shine like torches. That's what makes it so easy to spot, especially at night. If you happen upon one, don't waste any time: run immediately the other way!

You have no excuse now.
A keeper forewarned . . .

# Final Test
## to Become a Fantastic Beast Keeper

So here we are at the final test, the same one all Trainees
have to take to become full-fledged Keepers.
No need to worry: if you've read all my notes carefully, you'll sail through it.

Ready?
Let's begin!

**1** What do you call a winged unicorn?

- A) Feathercorn
- B) Alicorn
- C) Flycorn

**2** Which of these words best describes a carbuncle?

- A) Shiny
- B) Crotchety
- C) Finicky

**3** Why can't an alicanto fly?

- A) Its wings are too small.
- B) Its head is too big.
- C) It's too heavy.

**4** Which kind of bird-like beast causes storms?

- A) Stormbird
- B) Lightningbird
- C) Thunderbird

**5** The cerberus is an excellent . . . ?

- A) Guard dog
- B) Retriever
- C) Truffle dog

**6** What is the largest number of tails a kitsune can have?

- A) Seven
- B) Nine
- C) Five

**7** The peluda got its name because it is . . . ?

- A) Hairy
- B) Poisonous
- C) Rude

**8** Which beast has a serpent for a tail?

- A) Griffin
- B) Baku
- C) Chimera

**9** Where does an ahuizotl live?

- A) On the branches of the tallest trees
- B) In underground tunnels
- C) In underwater caverns

**10** Which of these creatures does NOT breathe fire?

- A) Phoenix
- B) Peluda
- C) Chimera

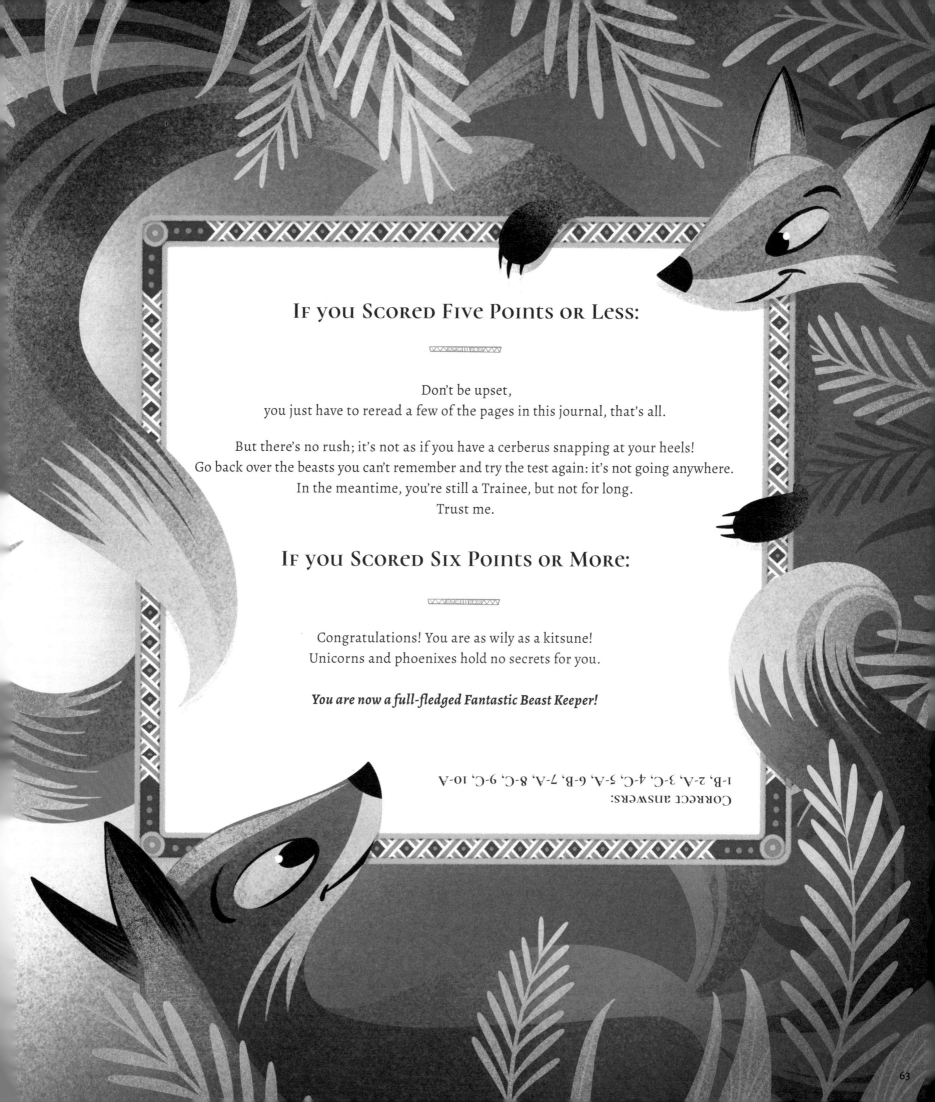

## If you Scored Five Points or Less:

Don't be upset,
you just have to reread a few of the pages in this journal, that's all.

But there's no rush; it's not as if you have a cerberus snapping at your heels!
Go back over the beasts you can't remember and try the test again: it's not going anywhere.
In the meantime, you're still a Trainee, but not for long.
Trust me.

## If you Scored Six Points or More:

Congratulations! You are as wily as a kitsune!
Unicorns and phoenixes hold no secrets for you.

***You are now a full-fledged Fantastic Beast Keeper!***

Correct answers:
1-B, 2-A, 3-C, 4-C, 5-A, 6-B, 7-A, 8-C, 9-C, 10-A

## Giuseppe D'Anna

Giuseppe D'Anna was born and raised in sunny Sicily and trained to be a graphic designer and artist in the hills of Tuscany. He currently lives here and there (as well as sometimes everywhere) and occasionally has fun writing books for children and young adults.

## Anna Láng

Anna Láng is a Hungarian graphic designer and illustrator who is currently living and working in Sardinia. After attending the Hungarian University of Fine Arts in Budapest, she graduated as a graphic designer in 2011. She worked for three years with an advertising agency, at the same time working with the National Theatre of Budapest. In 2013 she won the award of the city of Békéscsaba at the Hungarian Biennale of Graphic Design with her Shakespeare Poster series. At present she is working passionately on illustrations for children's books.

**STERLING CHILDREN'S BOOKS**
New York

An Imprint of Sterling Publishing Co., Inc.
1166 Avenue of the Americas
New York, NY 10036

ISBN 978-1-4549-4113-2

Distributed in Canada by Sterling Publishing
c/o Canadian Manda Group, 664 Annette Street
Toronto, Ontario, Canada M6S 2C8

For information about custom editions, special sales, and premium and corporate purchases, please contact Sterling Special Sales at 800-805-5489 or specialsales@sterlingpublishing.com.

Manufactured in Italy
Lot #:
2  4  6  8  10  9  7  5  3  1
07/20

sterlingpublishing.com

Translation: Denise Muir
Editing: Karen Levy